Welcome to **ALADDIN QUIX!**

If you are looking for fast, fun-to-read stories with colorful characters, lots of kid-friendly humor, easy-to-follow action, entertaining story lines, and lively illustrations, then **ALADDIN QUIX** is for you!

But wait, there's more!

If you're also looking for stories with tables of contents; word lists; about-the-book questions; 64, 80, or 96 pages; short chapters; short paragraphs; and large fonts, then **ALADDIN QUIX** is *definitely* for you!

ALADDIN QUIX: The next step between ready to reads and longer, more challenging chapter books, for readers five to eight years old.

Read all the ALADDIN QUIX books!

By Stephanie Calmenson

Our Principal Is a Frog!
Our Principal Is a Wolf!
Our Principal's in His Underwear!
Our Principal Breaks a Spell!

Royal Sweets
By Helen Perelman

Book 1: *A Royal Rescue*
Book 2: *Sugar Secrets*
Book 3: *Stolen Jewels*

A Miss Mallard Mystery
By Robert Quackenbush

Dig to Disaster
Texas Trail to Calamity
Express Train to Trouble
Stairway to Doom
Bicycle to Treachery
Gondola to Danger
Surfboard to Peril
Taxi to Intrigue

Little Goddess Girls
By Joan Holub and Suzanne Williams

Book 1: *Athena & the Magic Land*
Book 2: *Persephone & the Giant Flowers*

Little
GODDESS
Aphrodite & the Gold Apple
Girls

JOAN HOLUB &
SUZANNE WILLIAMS

ALADDIN QUIX

New York   London   Toronto   Sydney   New Delhi

ALADDIN QUIX
Simon & Schuster Children's Publishing Division
1230 Avenue of the Americas, New York, New York 10020
First Aladdin QUIX paperback edition January 2020
Text copyright © 2020 by Joan Holub and Suzanne Williams
Illustrations copyright © 2020 by Yuyi Chen
Also available in an Aladdin QUIX hardcover edition.
All rights reserved, including the right of reproduction in whole or in part in any form.
ALADDIN and the related marks and colophon are
trademarks of Simon & Schuster, Inc.
For information about special discounts for bulk purchases, please contact
Simon & Schuster Special Sales at 1-866-506-1949
or business@simonandschuster.com.
The Simon & Schuster Speakers Bureau can bring authors to your live event. For more
information or to book an event contact the Simon & Schuster Speakers Bureau
at 1-866-248-3049 or visit our website at www.simonspeakers.com.
Book designed by Tiara Iandiorio
The illustrations for this book were rendered digitally.
The text of this book was set in Archer Medium.
Manufactured in the United States of America 1219 OFF
2 4 6 8 10 9 7 5 3 1
Library of Congress Cataloging-in-Publication Data
Names: Holub, Joan, author. | Williams, Suzanne, 1953- author. | Chen, Yuyi (Artist),
illustrator. | Title: Aphrodite & the gold apple / by Joan Holub and Suzanne Williams;
illustrated by Yuyi Chen. | Other titles: Aphrodite and the gold apple
Description: First aladdin paperback edition. | New York : Aladdin, 2020. | "Aladdin
QUIX." | Summary: Eight-year-olds Aphrodite, Athena, and Persephone continue their
journey on the Hello Brick Road to meet Zeus and meet a new, timid friend, Artemis.
Identifiers: LCCN 2019020642 (print) | LCCN 2019022032 (eBook) |
ISBN 9781534431133 (eBook) | ISBN 9781534431119 (pbk) | ISBN 9781534431126 (hc)
Subjects: LCSH: Aphrodite (Greek deity)—Juvenile fiction. | CYAC: Aphrodite (Greek
deity)—Fiction. | Goddesses, Greek—Fiction. | Mythology, Greek—Fiction. | Fantasy.
Classification: LCC PZ7.H7427 (eBook) | LCC PZ7.H7427 Apf 2020 (print) | DDC [E]—dc23
LC record available at https://lccn.loc.gov/2019020642

Cast of Characters

Aphrodite (af•row•DYE•tee):
A golden-haired, beautiful girl
found in a shell

Athena (uh•THEE•nuh): A
brown-haired girl who travels to
magical Mount Olympus

Persephone (purr•SEFF•oh•nee):
A girl with flowers and leaves
growing in her hair and on her
dress

Oliver (AH•liv•er): Athena's
puppy

Zeus (ZOOSS): Most powerful of the Greek gods, who lives in Sparkle City and can grant wishes

Hestia (HESS•tee•uh): A small, winged Greek goddess who helps Aphrodite, Athena, and Persephone

Medusa (meh•DOO•suh): A mean mortal girl with snakes for hair, whose stare can turn other mortals to stone

Artemis (AR•tih•miss): A black-haired girl with a bow and arrow

Contents

Chapter 1: On the Road   1

Chapter 2: Medusa's Poppies 13

Chapter 3: Up the Mountain   31

Chapter 4: Artemis   43

Chapter 5: Sparkle City   56

Chapter 6: The Gold Apple 70

Word List   82

Questions   85

Authors' Note   87

1

On the Road

Aphrodite rolled her neck from side to side. *Swish* went her long golden hair. Then she circled her arms in the air. "Feels *sooo* good to be able to stretch," she told **Athena** and **Persephone**. She had met these two new friends only yesterday here in the magical land of **Mount Olympus**. Both were eight years old, like her.

Because of a magic spell, she'd been locked inside a giant shell. She hadn't been able to move around much. So no wonder stretching felt good to her! Her new friends had rescued her from that shell in a deep underground place called **Wunderworld**.

After leaving that place they'd walked a long way along the

orange, blue, and pink Hello Brick Road. They had slept under the stars. Then they had gotten up early this morning to begin walking again. For the past two hours Aphrodite had made a game out of trying to step only on the pink bricks. Pink was her favorite color!

Persephone yawned. "All this walking is making me tired. If you showed me to a flower bed, I'd take a nap in a snap!"

Real leaves and flowers always grew from her dress. And from her curly yellow hair. So yesterday in Wunderworld some giant daisies had mistaken her for one of them. They'd tried to capture her! They'd wanted her to hang out and be friends with them forever. Luckily Aphrodite and Athena had been able to rescue her.

"At least **Oliver** is getting a nap. He's pooped," said Athena. She glanced down at Oliver, her little white dog. She was carrying him in her book bag. The top flap was open. His head stuck out, but his big brown eyes were closed. "The sooner we get to Sparkle City, the better. **Zeus** just *has* to help me get back home!" Athena said.

Aphrodite knew Athena didn't belong in this magical land. A strange storm had blown her here from far away.

"And I hope he'll give *me* the gift of good luck!" Persephone added. She was sure she had a case of "bad luck-itis." And she was afraid her bad luck rubbed off on others.

"Yeah, good plan," Aphrodite told Persephone as she **trudged** along. Having daisies try to trap you was definitely bad luck.

The three girls were on their way to see Zeus. He was king of the **gods** and super-duper powerful. If anyone could help them, it would be him! However, he lived in Sparkle City at the top of Mount Olympus. They hoped they would get there by tonight.

Aphrodite took a big jump to land on the next pink brick. She had a reason for wanting to see Zeus too. People told her she was hard to like sometimes. Probably because she said whatever words came into her head, without thinking first. And sometimes that hurt people's feelings or made trouble. So she wanted Zeus to give her the gift of **likability**. Then maybe she'd be able to make and *keep* friends.

She looked at the sleeping dog. "I wish *I* was small enough to fit inside your book bag," she said to Athena. "Then maybe I could catch some z's too!"

Athena and Persephone laughed. The Hello Brick Road had been winding up a grassy hill for the past twenty minutes. Now they got to the top of it.

"Look! Poppies!" Persephone exclaimed. She pointed ahead. Fields of bright red flowers grew on both sides of the road far into the distance. Giggling in delight, she left the road and went leaping through the flowers.

"No!" Athena quickly called out. "Come back!" She chased Persephone into the poppy field, trying to stop her.

Hestia, a tiny, glowing, fairy-like **goddess**, had told them that as long as they stayed on the Hello Brick Road they would be safe. But there was danger once off it. The last time they'd seen the tiny goddess, she'd said: "If all goes well, you'll reach Sparkle City soon. But there's danger ahead. Watch out for—"

Only before she could tell them what they needed to watch out for, her glowing light began blinking. And then . . . *Pop!* She'd disappeared.

"Ha! Danger doesn't scare *me*!" Aphrodite had declared at the time. Even so, she didn't stray from the road. She just hoped that her friends weren't making a very bad mistake.

As she watched worriedly, both girls slowed and then sank to their knees. "Sooo sleepy," Persephone murmured.

Athena yawned. "Me too." They lay down among the poppies and began to snore softly.

"Wake up!" Aphrodite called from the safety of the road. But the two girls stayed fast asleep.

Suddenly Aphrodite heard a familiar cackle. *"Eee-heh-heh!"* A girl with wiggly green snakes for hair popped up from behind a tall clump of poppies near Athena.

"**Medusa**!" Aphrodite exclaimed, frowning. She was the one who'd used magic to trap Aphrodite in that shell!

2

Medusa's Poppies

"That's my name, don't wear it out!" Medusa gave Aphrodite an evil grin. This snake-haired girl could turn people to stone. She did it with magic zaps from her eyes. Those zaps hadn't worked the time she tried them on Aphrodite, though. So she'd locked her in that shell instead.

"Go away forever and I promise I'll never say your name again," Aphrodite blurted out. As usual, she spoke without thinking.

"Grr," growled Medusa.

"Hisss," went her snakes.

Aphrodite pointed toward her sleeping friends. "You cast a spell over those poppies, didn't you? So they'll make everyone but you take a nap!"

"That's right," said Medusa. "You snooze, you lose. In Athena's case anyway. Watch this!" She waved her arms over the poppies. "Army, rise up!" she shouted.

At once, large animal-shaped stones appeared out of nowhere. They stood in rows like animal soldiers. There were life-size monkeys, deer, wolves, bears, giraffes, hippos, and more!

Aphrodite's eyes got big. "Did you eye-zap a whole zoo, or what?"

Medusa ignored her. Instead,

she called out to the stone animals. "Carry the girl with the little white dog back to my castle."

The animal army began to move. **Stomp. Stomp. Stomp.** They chanted a song as they marched toward Athena:

"*Once we were animals. Now we are stone.*

"*Changed by Medusa who rules from her throne.*

"*All of her orders we must obey.*

"*We do what she tells us to, day after day.*"

Aphrodite wanted to help Athena and Persephone. But she did not want to leave the Hello Brick Road. If she ran into the poppy field, she'd just fall asleep too. Somehow she had to **foil** Medusa's plan.

She thought fast. "If it's Athena's magic sandals you're after, maybe *I* can get them for you," she said. "Then you won't *need* to take her to your castle."

Medusa had been after those sandals ever since that storm had blown Athena here. The sandals had white wings at their heels and could fly. Medusa claimed they were *hers*. Yet they'd slid onto Athena's feet and seemed quite happy to stay there.

"Nice try," Medusa replied. "But I know only Athena can take them off. And once I've locked her in my castle, she'll give them to me. Or I won't let her leave."

Aphrodite crossed her fingers behind her back. Then she told a fib. "Athena lets me and Persephone borrow her sandals all the time. It's easy as pie for us to pull them off her feet and fly them!"

Medusa's eyebrows shot up in surprise. "Army, halt!" she called out. The stone animals froze in their tracks. She looked at Aphrodite and nodded toward the sandals. "Go get them, then."

"No way!" said Aphrodite. "Those poppies will make me sleep too."

"Not if I make a path through them," said Medusa. At her order, a stone bear, a hippo, and a large monkey stomped off, clearing a path. It began a few inches from Athena and ended where Aphrodite stood on the road. "There," said Medusa. "Happy now?"

"Nope," said Aphrodite. "How do I know that path is safe?"

"You are *sooooo* annoying!"

grumped Medusa. "I wish you'd never gotten out of that shell." She pointed at Oliver. "Get that dog and set him on the path," she commanded the monkey.

"Eep! Eep!" went the monkey statue. It did as she ordered. Right away the little dog woke. **"Woof! Woof!"**

Aphrodite clapped her hands and called, "Come, Oliver!" He paused and looked over at the sleeping Athena. But then he ran down the newly cleared path to Aphrodite. "Good boy!" She scooped him up in her arms.

Medusa frowned. Her snakes flicked their forked tongues. "Stop **stalling**," she told Aphrodite. "He stayed awake. You got your proof. Now go get me those sandals!"

"Whoa. You're so impatient!" Aphrodite set Oliver on the Hello Brick Road. "Stay," she told him. "You'll be safe here." Luckily, the little dog obeyed.

Aphrodite hurried down the cleared, poppy-less path. When she came even with Persephone, she stopped. "Um . . . I just remembered something," she said, hoping to fool Medusa. "I need Persephone's help to get the sandals."

"**What?** Why?" Medusa demanded.

Quickly, Aphrodite came up with an answer. "Because I can only pull off Athena's left sandal. Persephone has to pull off the right."

This was another fib. Medusa had been right. Actually, no one but Athena could remove the sandals from her feet. Aphrodite shrugged. "Silly, isn't it? But, magic is weird, right? Like that eye zap thing you do."

"**Enough!** Just get on with it!" yelled Medusa. She motioned to the monkey statue. It tugged Persephone over to the cleared path.

Safe from the poppies' spell, Persephone woke up. She rubbed her eyes. "What happened?" she asked Aphrodite. "One minute I was running through the poppies, and the next minute—" Her words came to a stop. She had noticed Medusa snooping over Aphrodite's shoulder. Persephone pointed at the snake-haired girl. "What's *she* doing here?"

"She cast a spell over the

poppies that made you fall asleep. Athena, too," Aphrodite explained. "But once we give her Athena's magic sandals, she'll go away and leave us alone. C'mon. I'll pull off the left sandal while you pull off the right one."

Persephone jumped to her feet. "But we can't do that, because . . ."

Aphrodite butted in in a flash. "Because Hestia told us we shouldn't let Medusa have them? That she might use their magic to make trouble for Mount Olympus?"

"Well, yes," Persephone said.

"Baloney," Aphrodite replied. "Hestia worries too much. I'm sure Medusa will only use the sandals to do *good* magic." She winked big at Persephone.

Medusa didn't see the wink. "Sure, only *good* magic! *Eee-heh-heh*," the snaky girl fib-cackled.

At last Persephone caught on. She grinned at Aphrodite. "Oh. Then I guess it's okay."

The girls moved to the end of the path. They bent over Athena's feet. Aphrodite grasped Athena's left sandal. Persephone grasped her right one. Then, to **distract** Medusa, Aphrodite looked over at the stone army animals. "Hey, why is that hippo hula dancing?"

Medusa whipped around. **"Behave, or else!"** she shouted to her stone animals. But they were all standing at attention, including the hippos.

"Pull!" Aphrodite whispered to Persephone. Holding tight to Athena's feet, the two girls dragged her to safety on the path. The sleeping spell broke, and Athena opened her eyes. Aphrodite and Persephone grabbed her hands and tugged her to stand.

"Run!" Aphrodite shouted. Holding hands, the three girls raced down the path toward the Hello Brick Road as fast as they could go.

3

Up the Mountain

"After them!" Medusa shouted to her army. But Aphrodite, Persephone, and Athena could run faster than heavy stone statues. Within seconds, the three friends got to the Hello Brick Road. *Safe!*

Oliver leaped into Athena's arms. **"Woof!"** She hugged him.

"You tricked me!" Medusa shrieked. She shook her fists at the girls. Her snakes hissed. They flicked their forked tongues.

"So? You were going to *kidnap* Athena!" Aphrodite replied.

"Huh?" said Athena as Oliver licked her cheek. "She was?"

Aphrodite nodded. "She was going to lock you up in her castle and keep you there until you gave her your winged sandals."

Persephone gasped. She stared at Medusa. "I knew you were up to no good!"

Athena looked at her sandals. Then she looked over at Medusa. The snake-haired meanie was stomping around the poppy field.

"I'll never let you get these sandals," Athena called to her. **"Never, ever!"**

"So you say *now*," Medusa muttered. She angrily plucked petals off poppies and tossed them to the wind. "But you'll change your mind. Those sandals have powers you can't even guess. Only *I* know what magic they can do."

"All the more reason for Athena to keep them!" Aphrodite said. "Come on," she told her two friends. "Let's try to reach Sparkle City before dark." To Medusa, she said, "You can take your mean old army and march on back to your castle."

"Yeah," said Persephone. "You can't harm us. Not as long as we stick to the road!"

"Eee-heh-heh!" cackled

Medusa. "You haven't seen the last of me! Army, **retreat**!" she ordered her statues. Immediately, they disappeared without a trace. Then she went too, in a puff of green smoke. *Poof!*

Aphrodite punched a fist in the air. "Sparkle City, here we come!"

They walked for another hour, then came to the base of the steepest part of Mount Olympus. Athena pointed to the top of the mountain. "Look! Rainbow-colored sparkles!" They were from Sparkle City.

"Almost there!" Persephone exclaimed. "We just have to climb the rest of this thing!"

"Too bad it's so steep," Athena remarked.

They started upward. Along the way they picked and munched on berries. Oliver ate them too. After a while they came to a very thick forest. It was dark inside it. So dark they could barely see the road ahead. Animal sounds made them jump. So did scraping tree branches.

"Hoot!" "Growl!"

Scritch-scratch!

"I wish we had a flashlight," whispered Athena. At her words, the girls heard a click. The single wing at the back of each of Athena's sandals began to glow. The glow was so bright it lit the girls' way!

Aphrodite grinned at Athena. "I think you just found out another one of your sandals' magic powers! Besides flying, I mean."

Suddenly Oliver's ears perked up. He

began to growl and bark. Then he dashed up the road.

"Oliver! Come back!" Athena shouted. But this time the little dog didn't obey.

The girls raced after him. **"Woof! Woof!"** Oliver came to a stop at the base of a big olive tree. Here, the Hello Brick Road made a half-circle around the tree before continuing straight ahead again.

Oliver stood on his hind legs. He pawed at the trunk. **"Grrr!"**

"G-get that wild animal away f-from m-me!" a frightened voice wailed.

The three girls **huddled** close together. "Is that tree talking?" Athena whispered.

"Maybe," Aphrodite said. "Many things talk in this land."

"Yeah, remember those talking daisies in Wunderworld?" added Persephone.

Athena nodded. "Right. And a signpost on this very road spoke to me once. I'll just check this out." She lifted one sandaled foot into the air. When its glowing wing shone way up into the tree, the girls gasped.

"There!" Aphrodite pointed to a branch high up.

Standing on the branch was a girl about their age. Her long black hair hung over her shoulder in a single braid. She held a bow fitted with a silver arrow. The bow's string was pulled back tight. And the tip of the arrow was aiming down. At Oliver!

4

Artemis

"Stop!" yelled Athena. **"Don't hurt my dog!"**

Her shout startled the girl in the tree, just as Oliver's barking had. Her feet slipped on the branch.

As the girl tried to keep from

falling, she lost control of her bow. It swung to point upward. Her silver arrow shot through the air. **Zzzing!** It sailed through the branches high overhead.

Athena ran to Oliver. He was still barking at the tree. She hugged him. "You're safe now."

"Shame on you!" Aphrodite scolded the girl in the tree. "You could have *killed* Athena's dog!"

To everyone's surprise, the girl broke into sobs. "I didn't w-want to h-hurt him. I was just afraid h-he was going to climb the tree and b-bite me!"

"Dogs can't climb trees," Persephone informed her. "Besides, Oliver would never bite anyone!" Athena insisted.

"Except possibly Medusa," Aphrodite noted.

"M-Medusa?" The girl stopped crying but turned pale. She glanced around. "She's not h-here?"

"No," said Aphrodite. Softening a little, she added, "Why don't you climb down so we can talk?"

"I c-can't!" the girl wailed.

"I'll hold Oliver so he doesn't jump on you," Athena promised.

The tree girl tugged nervously on her braid. "If I let go of this branch, I'm afraid I'll f-fall!"

Aphrodite rolled her eyes. "Is there anything you're *not* afraid of?" she called up to the scaredy-girl. The minute the words left her lips she felt sorry for saying them. Zeus just *had* to give her the gift of likability. Then maybe she'd stop blurting out stuff like that!

Luckily, the scaredy-girl didn't mind. "N-not much. I'm p-pretty much afraid of e-everything."

"I'm scared sometimes too," Athena told her. "I remember I was *really* scared when I first got whooshed to this magic land. But everything's going to be okay." She handed Oliver to Persephone.

Her sandals' wings flapped as she lifted off the ground. Quickly, she flew up through the branches.

Aphrodite knew those magic sandals could fly. But until now she hadn't seen them in action. Wow! She wished *she* had sandals like that. Or something else magical.

"Take my hand," Athena said, reaching out to the scaredy-girl. "My sandals are strong enough to fly both of us."

"Are you s-sure?" the girl asked.

"It's true," Persephone said.

"They flew Athena and me all the way down to Wunderworld."

Still the girl **clung** to the tree. "I d-don't know."

Stop being such a **wimp**, Aphrodite almost said. But she stopped herself just in time.

"How about if *I* fly up there with Athena? Then will you believe the sandals are strong enough for two?" She did want to help. But mostly she wanted to fly!

"M-maybe," said the girl.

With that, Athena swooped down. Aphrodite grabbed her hand and was whisked high into the air. **"Whee! This is fun!"** she exclaimed. And it was! Athena flew her once around the tree. All too soon they landed.

"See? Nothing to it," Aphrodite

told the girl. She wished the flight had been longer.

Finally the girl's fear eased. "Okay. I'll t-try it," she told Athena.

Again, Athena flew up into the tree. The scaredy-girl hung her bow over one shoulder. Then she clasped Athena's hand. Seconds later, they were safe on the ground.

"Thanks for the ride." The scaredy-girl smiled at the others. "I'm **Artemis**."

The three friends gave their names too. "If you let Oliver sniff your hand, he'll know you're a friend," Athena told the girl.

After some **hesitation**, Artemis did just that. "Oh, look. He wagged his tail!" she said in delight. She even petted Oliver as Persephone went on holding him.

Just then Aphrodite remembered the girl's arrow. She went to search around the tree's roots for it. She figured Artemis might want it back. It was pretty dark here. But a little sunlight came through the trees. Enough to spot a gleam of silver in the grass.

"Gotcha!" she said, grabbing the arrow. "Hey, what's this?" A round, shiny object also lay on the ground. She picked it up. It was a tiny apple no bigger than a walnut. And it was made of real gold. *Huh?*

It couldn't have grown on the olive tree, could it? She looked upward. For a second she thought she saw a tiny blinking light among the tree's branches.

"Hestia?" Aphrodite called out.

But the light blinked off. Had she imagined it? She didn't see any more apples on the tree. Or on the ground. So where had this tiny apple come from? Could it be magic?

"Aphrodite, what are you doing?" Athena called to her. "We need to get going if we hope to reach Sparkle City tonight!"

"Coming!" Aphrodite called out. She put the gold apple into her pocket. Then she joined the other three girls. "Here. I found this," she said, handing the silver arrow to Artemis.

Artemis grinned. "Thanks!"

"You're very welcome," said Aphrodite. She thought about showing the others the gold apple. But something made her keep it a secret. She'd found the apple, so that meant it was *hers*. And if it turned out that the tiny apple had magic, well then, that magic would be hers too! There was nothing wrong with that, was there?

5

Sparkle City

"Guess what?" Persephone said to Aphrodite now that the girls were all together again. "Artemis is coming with us to Sparkle City to see Zeus!"

Aphrodite frowned. "Why?"

she asked. *Uh-oh.* That had sounded a bit rude. But really, she was worried. How many gifts could Zeus give out? Would adding one more person mean she might not get her gift? Still, she tried to be nice. "I mean, that's great, right?" **"Right!"** agreed Athena and Persephone.

As the girls started up the road again, those two took the lead. So Aphrodite walked next to Artemis. Oliver trotted alongside them all. Now and then he stopped to sniff the flowers they passed. Athena's sandals' glowing wings lit their way until the forest grew less thick.

"Persephone told me she's going to ask Zeus to give her the gift of good luck," Artemis told Aphrodite. "And Athena is going to ask him to help her get home. Since he's king of the gods and super-duper powerful, I'm hoping he'll grant me a gift too."

"Like what?" Aphrodite asked.

"The gift of **courage**. I'm tired of being afraid of everything." Artemis smiled at Aphrodite. "What are you going to ask for?"

"The gift of, um, likability." Aphrodite sort of mumbled that last word. It was embarrassing to admit that people didn't like her.

"Likability?" said Artemis. She

sounded surprised. "But you're *already* likable. I mean you were so kind about flying with Athena. To show me I shouldn't be afraid."

"Thanks," said Aphrodite. But, of course, she hadn't really acted out of kindness. She'd mostly wanted to try flying.

"Plus you found my silver arrow for me," Artemis went on. She patted the feathered end of the arrow. It was in a long thin pouch she carried over one shoulder.

Aphrodite guessed she *could*

take some credit for that. But then she remembered the gold apple she was keeping a secret. She wanted its magic (if it had any) to be all hers. Was that the act of a kind and likable person?

The girls kept on walking. Finally Athena called out, **"Look!"**

Aphrodite and the others gasped. Because there before them stood . . . Sparkle City!

A gleaming tower shaped like a giant thunderbolt and lit by

sparkling lights stood at the city's center. Roads stuck out from the base of the tower like spokes on a wagon wheel. Along them stood tidy little shops and houses of

various shapes and sizes. They were painted all the colors of the rainbow.

Happy, smiling people were everywhere. Some were walking. Others riding in colorful chariots pulled by horses or leopards. Still more rode upon the backs of fantastic creatures. Like enormous peacocks, and even dragons puffing rainbow-colored smoke!

They were *sooo* close to getting Zeus to grant their wishes! One big, tall problem though. Sparkle City was surrounded by a high glass wall dotted with sparkly jewels!

"Sparkle City is amazing!" Athena said with excitement.

"So shiny!" Persephone gushed.

"And not at all scary," Artemis added in relief.

"True," agreed Aphrodite. "But how do we get in?"

"No problem," said Athena. "Have you forgotten my winged sandals? I'll just *fly* us over this wall." She glanced down at her sandaled feet, then frowned. "Their wings have stopped glowing."

"Maybe because of all the light from the city?" Persephone guessed. "They didn't start glowing till it got dark in the forest before, remember?"

Athena nodded. "Yeah, maybe. That would make sense." She looked around at the others. "What if I take you over one at a time? My sandals might not handle the weight of more."

"Ooh! Take me second," Artemis begged. "Going first is scary, and going last would be even scarier.

I'd have to wait here alone!"

Aphrodite was about to say she would go first. But then she remembered the gold apple in her pocket. If keeping the apple a secret was an unlikable thing to do, so was asking to go first. "I can go last," she said.

"Okay, then I'll go first," Persephone volunteered.

"Great!" Athena smiled and tucked Oliver into her book bag again. Persephone grabbed her other hand. They waited for the sandals' wings to begin flapping. But they didn't.

"Maybe you need to *tell* them to fly?" Artemis suggested.

"I've never needed to before," said Athena. "But I'll try it." She looked down at her sandals. **"Fly, wings, fly!** Take us up and over this wall!" Nothing happened.

Behind them the girls heard laughter. They whirled around. A boy was walking toward them. He was outside the glass wall too.

He pointed at Athena's feet. "Zeus, the super-duper powerful god of Mount Olympus, cast a spell on the city wall to keep out troublemakers. Not even magic sandals will fly you inside."

"Troublemakers? Like Medusa, you mean?" asked Aphrodite.

The boy **flinched**.

"I'll take that as a 'yes,'" she said.

"We are not troublemakers," Athena protested. "And we've traveled a long way to get here."

"We just want to talk to Zeus,"

Persephone explained. "To ask for
his help."

"Huh?" said the boy. "No one
I know has ever even *seen* Zeus.
Much less talked to him!"

The Gold Apple

The four girls were stunned by this news. They stared at the boy.

"Well, good luck!" he told them. He went over to the wall. Humming a tune, he walked through the glass as if it wasn't even there.

"**Wait!**" Aphrodite called after him. "How did you get in?"

Turning, the boy held up a small gold apple. It looked exactly like the one in her pocket! He shouted something then, but she couldn't hear him through the wall. And before she could ask him to speak louder, he ran off.

The daisies in Persephone's flowery hair drooped sadly. "I'm sorry," she told the others. "I must have brought us bad luck."

"Baloney," said Aphrodite. She

pulled the gold apple from her pocket.

The others stared at it, open mouthed. "Where did you get that?" Athena asked.

"It was behind the tree where I found Artemis's silver arrow," Aphrodite admitted. "I think Hestia must have left it for us, because I saw a blinking light in the tree. But the light disappeared before I could talk to her." She blushed. "I should have told you about it right away, but I—"

"No problem," Athena interrupted. "The important thing is that you have it."

"Yeah!" Persephone said happily. The daisies in her hair sprang back up. "Now we just have to figure out how to use it to get us into the city."

Aphrodite tried pressing the apple against the glass wall. Nothing happened. "Listen up, apple.

I command you to let us into Sparkle City!" she tried. Nope. Still nothing.

"Maybe there's a secret space inside the apple that holds a key?" Artemis said shyly.

Huh? That's a dumb idea! Aphrodite almost blurted. She pressed her lips tightly together. That way no unkind words could escape. The apple felt solid. Plus, it was too small to hold a key. Besides, there was no door with a lock to put a key!

Still, Artemis is sweet, thought Aphrodite. She'd said Aphrodite was *very* likable. And kind, too! So she would be kind back and give her a chance. "Here," she said, handing Artemis the apple. "Why don't you take a look?"

Artemis took the apple. She turned it over and over in her hands. She tried pressing on it here and there, but nothing changed. She didn't give up, though. She poked a finger at the little stem at the top of the apple. "I wonder . . ."

Pinching the stem between her thumb and forefinger, she pulled up on it. Click!

Suddenly to the girls' surprise, the gold apple hummed a tune. The same tune they'd heard when the boy passed through the wall. "Quick! Try pressing it against the wall again!" Athena called out.

Artemis's eyes had gone round. She gave the apple back to Aphrodite. "You d-do it," she said. Humming gold apples were one more thing that scared her! **"Wait!"** Persephone said to Aphrodite. "Let's have everyone hold on to you. That way, if this works, we should all be able to walk through together."

Artemis and Persephone held on

to one of Aphrodite's arms. Athena held on to the other. Then she pressed the apple against the glass wall. The tune sounded again. They all held their breath . . . and stepped forward.

Right away the glass began to ripple around them. It felt like a brisk wind was blowing. But then they passed through!

"We did it. We're inside Sparkle City!" Aphrodite whooped. She smiled at Artemis. "Good job figuring out about the stem."

Artemis smiled back at her. "Thanks."

Persephone spread her arms out. "Group hug!" she shouted. Before meeting these girls, Aphrodite would have said that group hugs were silly. But it really had taken a *group* effort to get to

Sparkle City. And it felt right to celebrate! She slipped the gold apple back into her pocket. Then she hugged her friends tight.

"Onward!" Athena shouted after the grinning girls broke apart.

"We can do this!" Aphrodite cheered.

"We'll get Zeus to meet with us, no matter what that boy said!" added Persephone.

Artemis's voice shook only a little as she replied, "R-right!"

"To the tower?" asked Aphrodite. **"To the tower!"** the others exclaimed.

And with that, the four happy friends marched toward Zeus's thunderbolt tower at the center of Sparkle City.

Word List

clung (KLUNG): Held on to something tightly

courage (KER•idge): Bravery

distract (diss•TRAKT): To draw attention away from something

flinched (FLINCHD): Made a sudden small jerk from fear or surprise

foil (FOYL): To keep someone or something from succeeding

goddess (GOD•ess): A girl or woman with magic powers

gods (GODZ): Boys or men with magic powers

Greek mythology (GREEK mith•AH•luh•jee): Stories people in Greece made up long ago to explain things they didn't understand about their world

hesitation (hez•ih•TAY•shun): A pause before saying or doing something

huddled (HUD•uhld): Crowded together closely

likability (like•uh•BILL•ih•tee): Being easy to like

Mount Olympus (MOWNT oh•LIHM•pus): Tallest mountain in Greece

retreat (ree•TREET): To draw back, go away

stalling (STAWL•ing): Delaying, slowing something down

trudged (TRUJD): Walked slowly and heavily

wimp (WIMP): A weak and fearful person

Wunderworld (WON•der•wurld): Underground home to Hades and Cerberus (called the Underworld in Greek mythology)

Questions

1. Sometimes Aphrodite says things that she is later sorry for saying. Have you ever done that? What do you think she could do to stop herself from saying things like that?

2. Aphrodite told some fibs to trick Medusa and rescue her friends from the poppy field. What were the fibs? Do you think telling these fibs was okay? Why or why not?

3. Artemis tells Aphrodite she is already likable. How does knowing what Artemis thinks of her change

how Aphrodite acts toward Artemis?

4. Aphrodite keeps the tiny gold apple she finds and doesn't tell her friends about it right away. Do you think that was fair of her?

5. What does each of the four girls do that helps them all finally get into Sparkle City?

6. Do you think Zeus will agree to see Athena, Persephone, Aphrodite, and Artemis and give them the gifts they are hoping for? Why or why not?

Authors' Note

Some of the ideas in the Little Goddess Girls books come from **Greek mythology.**

Aphrodite was the Greek goddess of love and beauty. A seashell was one of her symbols. She sometimes became jealous of others. When that happened, she could be quite bad-tempered!

Persephone was the Greek goddess of plants and flowers. Athena was the Greek goddess of wisdom. Artemis, skilled at archery, was the Greek goddess of animals and the moon.

We also borrowed a few ideas from *The Wonderful Wizard of Oz*, a book written by L. Frank Baum. In that book, there is a road called the Yellow Brick Road. In this book, there is a Hello Brick Road. There are other similarities too, including a poppy field that puts people and animals to sleep! We've also added lots of action and ideas of our own to this book.

We hope you enjoy reading the Little Goddess Girls books!

—*Joan Holub and Suzanne Williams*